PEARL OF TH

A fairytale prequel to 'Black Inked Pearl'

by

Ruth Finnegan

Pearl of the seas

© Ruth Finnegan 2016

A fairytale prequel to 'Black inked pearl'

ISBN 978-1-326-92926-8
Callender Press
125 Church Green Road, Old Bletchley

Remembering

ISIDORE OKPEWHO

a great and generous scholar of Africa

and a friend to all who love her.

Author's Note

I wish to offer my heartfelt thanks to all my readers, reviewers and critics, especially Denny Taylor and the marvellous team at Garn Press for their warm support and friendship. This has meant so much to me in both practical and emotional – I might even say spiritual – terms.

I would also like to thank my wonderful daughters and grandchildren who teach me what's what. I am still led by my memories of reading the Narnia tales to them and sharing their enjoyment; and of my own magical memories of Andrew Lang's many hue'd fairy books, the excitements of Rider Haggard and the Arabian Nights and, in a different mode, 'Swallows and Amazons' and 'Rolf in the Woods', all delights of my childhood.

The book is for the enjoyment of children of all ages. If this small tale brings anything of the same insight and joy I will indeed be happy. Long may The Pearl sail the great seas of mystery, magic and wisdom. And so may we all.

Old Bletchley, June 2016

Contents

"I saw three ships come sailing in,

On Christmas day, on Christmas day,

I saw three ships come sailing in,

On Christmas day in the morning.

And what[1] was in those ships all three?

On Christmas day, on Christmas day,

And what was in those ships all three?

On Christmas day in the morning.

Our Saviour Christ and his lady

On Christmas day, on Christmas day,

Our Saviour Christ and his lady,

On Christmas day in the morning …

And all the bells on earth shall ring,

On Christmas day, on Christmas day,

And all the bells on earth shall ring,

On Christmas day in the morning.

And all the Angels in Heaven shall sing,

On Christmas day, on Christmas day,

And all the Angels in Heaven shall sing,

On Christmas day in the morning"

Traditional

Here are our thoughts, voyagers' thoughts,

Here not the land, firm land, alone appears, may then by them be said,

The sky o'erarches here, we feel the undulating deck beneath our feet,

We feel the long pulsation, ebb and flow of endless motion,

The tones of unseen mystery, the vague and vast suggestions of the

*   briny world, the liquid-flowing syllables,*

The perfume, the faint creaking of the cordage, the melancholy rhythm,

The boundless vista and the horizon far and dim are all here,

And this is ocean's poem.

Walt Whitman, *Leaves of Grass*

Chapter 1 Seashore and dog

'Come on Kate,' shouted Chris, and whistled to Holly who was busily sniffing round the shells and beetles in the rocks at the edge of the shore, 'let's paddle',

'Okay. Hurry up then slowcoach,' Kate yelled back as she watched Chris slowly rolling up his battered tattered fading jeans.

'All right for you,' he grumbled, 'just a short skirt'.

But anyway he followed Kate into the wavelets at the water's edge, Holly in front of them both and under all their legs (*how do dogs do it, even the littlest ones?*). How Holly could *run* too - when the mood took her! (*she was a very clever little dog. And obedient too. Always. Except when - oh just except when she wasn't, you know what I mean*).

'Holly even easier,' retorted Kate.

So they all three splashed gleefully in the sea, Holly leaping high as the skies, the heavens, the heaping upon heaping heaps, leaping heaping sweeping, and higher still in gleeful flightful lightsome delighting delight. Barking, sparking, larking.

'Magic, isn't she,' whispered Kate.

Kate splashed Chris even bigger than she'd meant, then ran off giggling as the splash lashed dashed bashed him. Hard. So he pretended to chase her up the shore.

Next they decided to build a rampart against the sea. They knew all right that the springtime tide would top it, but that was all part of the fun. Chris did the heavy work. Of course. Kate, queen of the castle, sat on top of her ramparts and watched approvingly – yes she *was* the queen, of course - and the dirty rascal Chris (except he wasn't) stretched his full length on the sand ('Gosh he's grown,' thought Kate). Surely his length, strength, width, wiseness would keep off the waves?

Well, you know ... So did Kate, really. Up came a big wave and ... (*we don't need to tell you do we*).

Chris tried not to be cross - he'd been told off about that before. (*Well alright, he wasn't perfect, heroes seldom are. But nor was Kate, really. Just not in the same way as him (and just wait till we get to the counting bit)*). All Chris could do was wring the water out of his shirt. Try to. Kate tried to hide her smile (*all right for girlies, tight tee shirts, innit?*).

'Race you!' shouted Chris. And off he set up the shore before Kate could even get started (*cheat!*)

Not fair!

Yes, but look! He turned round, stopped suddenly at a halt, FULL STOP! holding his side and gasping like a - well whatever people gasp like when they're pretending ...

'Oh, *what* a stitch,' he gasped in pain (well ...).

So Kate won and leapt up and down in delight, Holly helping, yelping, yapping, hurray, soaking them both! Kate knew, really, but still ... Nice for a girl to win for once!

Chapter 2 'Pearl of the Sea' and bad-hat counting

' Kate Kate.' Chris's excited shout rang across the shore, even louder than the winding wind, the whistling breeze, the flustering fluttering wavelets., 'Quick quick, come quick'.

But Kate was deep in a fairytale novel full of dreams and did *not* want to be disturbed. And even when she wasn't reading, her secret vi- - well reading wasn't really a 'vice' was it whatever her mum said? More like a 'voice'. (*Oh there you go again Katey Kate, voices and vices and wises and songses, and three-sonicked word-fullnesses sound-ringing in her head - we'll just have to get used to it, you, so just – well, manage!*) - well when she wasn't reading it was good just to sit silent on the shore, scooping sand grains in her hands, falling them through her fingers, grain by grain, counted, countless. Or feeling the clouds and the moon, numbering the stars ...

Numbering? No! She had never been able to cope with numbers.

Yes you got it right. She'd never been any use with that. Not! That was the stuff she'd had to put up with at school before they were let out to play.

Yes she'd learnt her times-tables and grammar and maps of the world (*if only ...*) and pound shillings pence (*those were the bad old days, you know before thy had proper money. The magic days*). And today – *oh!!*).

'Now class, multiply 3679 by 107, add 13, think a bit, then take away 13, what have you got Kate?'

But Kate had forgotten to take away the 13, she'd added it all right but then ... oh *horrible* number. And they were all *laughing* at her! Ohh!

At least Chris wouldn't laugh so she'd better pay him some attention.

'Mmm? Oh it's you Chris. Well not now ... I'm reading. Lovely words ...'

That reminded her ...   (*off goes her mind again. Wool-gathering (wool, pull, fool, full gathering-ing ...). Yes, that was Kate for you!*).

She'd been in school trouble t'other day all right. Scratched on the loo wall. Again.

If you sprinkle

As you tinkle

Be a sweetie

Wipe the seatie.

Well, it was *good* advice, wasn't it? But no thanks did she get. Lines ! 'And this shall be your text: "I must not, must not never write four lines of dirty ditties on toilet walls when one, one will do. I must shun from all long verses, prose (prose!) must be lean and mean, I MUST NOT!" .'

Kate tried, she really did, and missed supper ('lean' indeed) to do it. And breakfast too if her mum'd allowed. For the first try didn't pass (she'd missed a 'not' in the second line).'The second didn't either, she'd counted wrong hadn't she now (*oh Kate, Kate*) and written it once too often (*oh Kate, numbers!*).

Oh well. Think about ships. 'I saw three, er one, ship a-sailing in ... '

Ohh!!

Kate's name on the redboard–sinboard! 'Miss Cath-erine to see Head *statim*, now. H.E.N.' Her full name. It was serious then. Called to Her-Eminence-Now High Excellent Mother Hen (how *dare* she take that scared-sacred mother-name).

'And what my dear' ('my dear' – it was *really* serious) 'would you say was your besetting sin? My dear?' she asked.

'Er. Er. Er. Too much reading, or er' (*what would sound good*) 'er, dreams.'

'No, my dearest lamb ' (*worse*) 'it is impatience. Im-pat-i-ence. And OverTheTopness' (Kate had never heard of that, not one of the Deadly sins, perhaps she only qualified for second-class ones and ...)

'*Attend.* IMPATI-ENCE. You skip to the end to see the finish and not stay for the middle, the meat.'

Kate hung her head. HeadWitch, er, HeadNun was right. Her sins were indeed scarlet (scarlet woman, scarlet, scartle, scampering scarletting scartling sacriletting, no, *sacrileging* down the ages, rages, sages, mages, wisemen, stars ....oh yes and Catherine's gridir'ning, wheeling, feeling, lightning, stabs, and fireworks er and -),

'Yes sister, no sister, *mea culpa culpissima* sister'. Run for it.

H.E.N hadn't mentioned her darning – not really her thing, didn't matter anyway (*how wrong she was. No darners inn heaven so she'd be <u>needed</u>. All'd gone down to the darn-, the dam-ned darning-ned dungeons below, where there was wailing and gnashing of teeth and much darning and dashing and socking of men's heads and heels – well heels would always need darners, even down there, wouldn't they*).

Strange – with all that there she couldn't quite help but love the teachers. Misguided all right ('*Miss Guided*', ha ha) – but that's education you know. Not like a ship, a ship, guided by the breath of the wind, couldn't wait to find one. Even just a boat.

'All right Chris, just a moment ... '

'Hurry up then, bin waiting ages. No trick. You'll love it'.

Kate shut her book pretend-reluctantly and walked slowly-quick-quick across the sand.

'Just *look.'* Chris was almost too excited to speak. ' Look look a *boat!* Building one, for ... '.

He was tugging at the end of a heavy piece of driftwood half-buried in the sand. 'Come on, help me'.

'A boat?' said Kate in disgust,' that dirty old log?'

Well when she looked at it, perhaps it did look a bit like a ship, with its branching out - oars were they? And that upstanding mast?

'And see here' said Chris. And he signalled with his eyes at a glowing flowing growing something on the sand at his feet. Great it was, burnished, like copper but not copper, wood-sweet and soft-hard, oak, and a cherry handle; polished and shining, shimmering, shingling in the sun, light high to the heavens the clouds the stars ... \what could it be?

'Made by my dad,' he said.

'Didn't know you had a dad,' said Kate thoroughly surprised, 'thought you just had a mum. Like me.'

''She went off years ago', said Chris gruffly. 'My dad, he's wonderful. Foster dad really', he explained, 'carpenter, designer, thinker. Joey. No one like him. ' Then, shyly, 'He says I'll be like him one day, have he eye for it, he'll teach me when I'm older. Next year. Says I'll do all right if I keep at it and don't go jauntering off all over the place.'

'But what *is* it?' persisted Kate, pointing at the Thing, but keeping her bare feet well away in case it bit.

'A rudder. A rudder. Tiller. He must have *known* we were planning a ship. Come *on* Kate, lets get on with it.'

So they tugged and pulled and heaved and hove. And Holly hove and step-tugged and panted and strained too, all four little paws firm planted in the sand, and turned her magic eye on the inert piece of wood.

And so for hours (*was it? But what are hours in eternity?*) they worked and struggled, and chopped and lopped and clawed and sawed (*and where did they find a saw and an axe on that long empty strand? Don't ask me about it, those were magic times you know. Or maybe Joey had slipped down to leave them his cast-off bits and pieces*),

And look look! The log dissolved and solved and resolved itself, and melted and curved, and toiled and coiled and moiled and furled. And was it, wasn't it (*look deep in Holly's magicalising eye*) it was it was it was - a *ship*! High mast, sails up and ready to go, flag atop mast fluttering in the wind. Magicked there.

Ready to take off.

'I'm going round the world in her,' said Chris. And the hero light shone from his eyes.

'What's the ship called?' asked Kate timidly (*she was totally overawed. Awesome. Cool!*)

'I'm calling her *Dragonfly*.'

'Funny. Why on earth?'

'Don't be slow Kate. She - ' (*she?*) will fly to the ends of the world and back. On dragon wings. Strong as the wind, Flames. Smoke. Enchanten-ment.'

'Why can't *I* name it, er, her too?' demanded Kate indignantly, 'worked just as hard.'

'What's your silly, er great idea then? Girls don't name ships anyway.'

'Pearl, of course she's Pearl. And I do, so there! I just *have!*'

'Dragon -.'

'Well Pearl at the back, Dragon at the. ... ,'

'Hey,' interrupted Chris, no respecter of persons, or of dogs either, 'hey then, " Ship on the sea", not bad. Maybe we'll have that.'

'Pearl, ' said Kate firmly, 'Pearl of the Seas.'

'Okay.' Chris knew when he was beaten, ' so long as there's Dragonfly on the stern.'

'Yes,' said Kate a little absently as another thought struck her. ' Are you *really* going round the world Chris? Ooh can I come too?'

Chris tried to look doubtful. *Of course!* He'd planned for that. Countiing on it.

'Yes,' he said. Graciously (*even if she wasn't too bright on numbers she let him boss her around and anyway he needed a crew. That's what girlies were for, wasn't it, being bossed around, and tell the truth she was better than most, couldn't go without her really.*)

'All right.'

And the Pearl was so *beautiful.*

"Look on this ship of God's creatures

And see how it is steeped in love"

Silence. .

'Must be wonderful to have a mum Kate. Cherish you. Sometimes I dream ... oh shut up, Kate, you're such a chatterbox, can't you see that big stone there, have you forgotten we need something for an anchor stupid. Oh *all* might, I'll carry it, you girlies all so *feeble*.'

Kate opened her mouth in surprise but shut again and got out of the way quick when she saw Chris's face and his kick at the sand which flew up in a great cloud and nearly buried poor Holly - well he had to conceal his feelings *somehow (it was himself he wanted to kick of course - how he could have let out ... oh but a mum to care for him. And for his dad, that was his ...)*.

'Oh *come on* Kate, we don't have all day ...'

He paused and looked at Kate, then at the ship.

'Oh Kate, ' in hushed awe, 'you're right, she *is* beautiful! Did *we* - really build her! it seems impossible ... '

Kate, whispering, equally awed, 'It must have been Holly helping, something magical anyway. And maybe', timidly, 'your dad? The skill you inherited from him I mean.'

Chris turned away abruptly. 'Oh dunno. Anyway let's try her out, okay?'

Followed by Holly the two clambered carefully aboard, trying to control the violent rocking - they're weren't much used to boats. Then with a few muddles and pushes, and 'helping' in-the-waynesses from Holly, they managed – *just* - to sit down, wobbly (*careful Kate*), and get the boat going.

The breeze was just the light helpful kind for beginners, it pushed them gently, didn't even need to wrestle with getting the sails up. Then - good or bad? - it died away completely *just* when they were in the middle of the lagoon. Kate looked horrified, but Chris just burst out laughing.

' What are oars for simpleton?'

Sure enough he pulled the oars from where they sat next to the rail - Kate was actually touching one of them already - and, unhandily at first, and then with amazing speed and skill, there they were bringing the ship smoothly in to the shore and beaching her. Gently, just right. Holly jumped off first, then the two of them, still laughing and clutching each other as they jumped wobbly onto the sand.

'Time for tea' said Kate reluctantly, don't really want to leave her ... '.

'Lucky you ' - Chris, *sotto voce*.

'Tomorrow then Chris? Another sail? She's terrific.'

'Sure thing. You'll see!'

'Ooh can't wait', cried Kate. 'But bother, teatime, me mam will be after me. And oh dear, school tomorrow. Oh but then - weekend. Bye now.'

Off raced Kate up the strand, Holly close behind.

Chris bent down to tie the ship gently to a stake he hammered into the sand. Couldn't be too careful. Then off he went to get his dad's tea.

The ship waited. She heard in the winds the song Orpheus once sung to his magic ship the Argo,

"How sweet it is

to ride upon the surges

to leap from wave to wave,

while the wind sings cheerful in the cordage,

and the oars flash fast among the foam!"

And the good ship heard the song *(is it not with us still? and with every ship on the land and the sea?)*, and longed to be away and out at sea; till she stirred in every timber, and heaved from stem to stern, and leapt up from the sand upon the rollers, and plunged onward like a gallant horse ready to rush into the whispering sea.

And so it was that the Pearl of the Seas gathered her sails and gazed after them, waiting to go.

Chapter 3 No!!

Saturday at last. Chris at the prow, sails floating to go. Gathering following wind. Perfect.

Up climbed Kate onto the stern. All in her best holey jeans she was. Just right for a crew. Holly was crew too of course, but not *essential* crew. Like Kate was.

Jeans not quite as holey as Chris's. But she was crew, not skipper.

On with Holly next. Bi-ig leap, oh good girl, well done. '*Sit.* Sit down!'

'Up with the mains'l Kate!' shouted Chris. Nautical talk. Skipper.

Didn't know how. But still – up it went, halfway. Great. Not too hard.

Then. Sudden.

'Chris, oh oh, Chris I – Chris, the teachers told me. I ... too young ... Not learned darning yet. Not proper. For the sails you know. '

All in a rush. Terrified.

'And me mam needs me you know, would be fright-ed for me.'

' I'm not coming!'

Off she jumped into the water. Abandoning.

The sail fell down, *hard*, right on top of Chris. The rudder flew out of his skipper's hands, knocking him hard on the chin. Holly slipped off into the sea.

Kate fled.

Chris! You can imagine! Hurt, fury, *rage! Girls!*

The boat toppled, slowly lowly, tipped, lay flat on the tide. But not before it had bounced on and off a jagged hole-ing rock (not that the skipper saw, she floated still. Just).

There she lay, his lovely ship. Lifeless. No Kate. No life-breath.

She had killed her. And Chris too.

Look he's thrown off the sail, twisted the prow. Bashed the tiller. Snatched Holly (*Kate's* Holly!) and dumped her in the bottom. Rage.

Hard shuttered face. She'd never seen him look like that. And because of *her* ... No farewells. Not one.

And Kate – Kate watching ...

Oh how the teachers had deceived her. Why had she listened to them for one *minute*, one atom. *Of course* she had to go. Chris *depended* on her. And - an adventure.

She'd thought he'd of argued. Sweetly. 'I just want you for your own sake Kate. Not for darning. Would love you to come. *Need* a girlie ... '

Oh she'd been so wrong, she *had* to go with him.

She rushed to the water-edge, yelled, snatched at a trailing rope, hung on for all she was worth, rope burning her hands ...

Words might help, she breathed them in her mind.

Slipping from fingers,
rough fibre on hands,
that are pulling and gripping
fumbling and rasping
 struggling and nipping,

twisting and slipping

,fading and grasping

going and going

and going

and

gone ...

No good.

Teachers all wrong, poetry didn't help; at all at all at all at all ...

Last try.

Kate yelled to Holly, pretending calm. Coaxlike. 'Here here, come to Kate. Come on come on. Treats. Walkies!!'

That would do it. And - and, oh, it did. It worked. It was working! That would bring him back. The ship too ... *And* she'd have Holly back to comfort her. Chris too. Games on the shore. Not as good as an adventure. But *something*.

In plunged the little dog, dearest Holly. Coming to her. Swimming. 'Come on come on, here here here Holly'. There she was in the briney salty brining brine, swimming swimming, little paws, Swim swim swim. Gulp. Sw-i-i-m.

Sw-i-i-i-m.

Oh oh , current too strong.

Sw-i-i-i-i-m.

Sw-i- i - ....

Holly was drowning ... There in front of her eyes, drowning - eyes going under, blue eye, drowning, wall eye, silky tuft on top head ju-ust above the horrid waves, drowning drowning ...

Oh Chris to rescue! Chris Chris! Plunging in. Swimming. Strong. Holly on shoulder.

Aaah. Safe.

Aaah.

But not to shore. Ship.

And Kate, Kate! Chris'd not swum for *her*.

One quick wave he made, then straight to sea, no look back. Him. Hurt he was, furious hurted, hurting, no look back. That Kate had *rejected* him, refused, *and* his ship. Just when he was needing her. His crew.

He wasn't in a sulk, no never, just just - righteously angry.

Well, he might go back if she was suitably sorry. Aahal. Yes! That would do it. But no. The wind. Carrying them out fast. To the wild sea.

Good thing. Really. He'd go it alone, didna need no help he didna.

Holly. Lying panting on the deck, she was, eyes shut. Forgetting. *Forgetting* her own Kate, changing sides ...

No Kate wasn't angry. She loved them both she did. Very very very much.

Very.

But oh how she *longed* - the one thing she wanted. The adventure. Not just that either. Not to let down her friend, her loyal friend, her loving loyal pal. Her own fault.

So Kate was left there.

Too late.

Chapter 4 Alone with the sky

Alone.

Ship smaller, going, smallest, slipping stealing stillen-ing sea-droppenly away.

Dolphins and whales leaping and winging round, in the sky, confusing.

Her not-her watching, turned away, unbearing.

The sail.

The mast.

The mast tip going ...

Then – just dolphins and whales leaping, only whales, only empty sky the only-sky, grey for joy that had gone, emptiness of sea.

Alone with the sky, the ever seeing sky. Chris. .

Sweet pinks, thrift-flowers of cliff and cloud. Harebells (how they had rung them in that olden faerie time). Why should they care?

Empty sea.

Gone.

As convolvulus roots dig deep in the earthe's heart, grown spiraling untwistable in th' ether till burst out in morning's glore

So Kate longed for their threesome voyaging.

As the starlight of the milken way that runs through the sky falls to the earth; as the spray of the wave mingles in sprung mist; as the tree feeds as one its branchen leaves and the birds of the sky

So should she have voyaged in that venturing together.

Kate tried to send a blessing after the ship, beautiful star of the sea (don't go, don't go, don't leave me).

Oh and herself, she could not speak for sobs, try again. She loved them loved them.

Oh moon oh shine,

Oh sink or swim,

Oh through the brine,

Oh keep thou him.

But her blessing caught in a snag of the rocks and didn't reach them.

And the ship – oh the ship, not even its masthead, its breath, its fragrancing. Vanished, vanished.

Gone.

Chapter 5   Yahwiel

Kate was sobbing her heart out.

And - 'Oh Holly Holly, what are you doing now?'

'Is Chris feeding you? Water? Hugging? And is Holly remembering K -   I can't say it ... '

An old man in a ragged tattered hat was hobbling across the sand.

Kate started to get up. She wondered how old he could be (very old ... maybe wise even) but she was *not* in the mood for talking. Go away.

But what was that? A sudden gust of wind? a sorry sigh from Kate?

Whatever it was it blew the old man's hat off into the water.

Kate turned her back. Not her business.

But well, maybe, perhaps, her mum had always told her 'Do as you would be done by'. Silly, she didn't have a hat, but there you were.

Deep breath to steady her, then raced, *raced* into the sea, just caught it as it was sinking before the fiercest magickest wave. Came back drenched.

'Here you are sir, your hat sir.'

'Yahwiel.'

'What??'

'Yahwiel. My name. Yahwiel the magician. But my dear child, why are you crying?"

"Oh oh no one can help me. My own fault.'

'Yes. Yes it was.'

'Said it was my mum. But really, ' draw deep breath, ' I was - was afraid. To go off like that. To sea. On my own.'

'Your own? '

'Well, felt like that.'

'Yes, my child, that was a fault indeed. But you can redeem yourself. Did you not help me with my hat?'

Kate looked at his hat. And see there, look, no longer a tattered battered wittered wetted crinkled bonnet - but a crown, gold with pearls and rubies, resplendent, filling the sky, the heavens with its glow, magical, entrancing Kate's eyes till she ...

But - 'Even the magickest magic can't help. Too late.'

'My child, you are wrong. For your kind deed, three riddles for you. If you can solve them, then are you in the boat with your dear friends. '

Little did Kate believe. But what else could she do. And anyway she had always been taught to be polite to old people and didn't want to offend one of them. Or hurt them (*that as the point wasn't it?*).

'All right then!'

'Pick up a grain of sand. Any one will do.'

Kate did so.

'Now. The riddle. What are holding in your hand?'

'A grain of sand (*silly!*). And, ' crossly, 'don't ask me to *count* it!'

She looked. And looked again. And like the hat - it grew, it flew it transformed itself, a pearl, the world, the world in a pearl ...

She looked, *felt,* across her answer. No words big enough.

'Now look again - the second. The heaven above you.'

Above her? No he was wrong. It was below beside her, around her. In her heart. *Through* her. And through the indigo glow, the rosy dawn the morning star of the sky she saw shining that lovely wild sorrel—white flower she had seen with her mother that morning, a century ago.

Yahwiel understood.

'You are right.'

'And now the third. The last. Can you riddle me it? The hardest and yet it is the easiest too. How many names has God?'

Counting!! She couldn't. Didn't he *know,* and he a magician, that she couldn't do numbers?

'Try,' said Yahwiel gently.

She couldn't, she couldn't. Despite herself she blurted (*oh how stupid. But what could she do? what but the truth?*)

'I - I don't know.'

She didn't know. She'd failed failed failed. She'd never see Holly again.

‗Or Chris. Never. And they'd sail the seas and be lost in a storm and sink and she wouldn't even be there to say goodbye. And ….

'Dear child,' said Yahwiel even more gently, 'you have done well. Your answers are indeed right. The world in a grain of sand. Heaven in a wild flower. And above all, the most precious flower, the world, the word, the wisest of all, wisdom from God himself "I don't know", the very fount of all wisdom.'

Not very dignified for the heroine of a fairytale but all Kate could do was stand there with her mouth open. What …

'And now,' he continued, 'after that sore trial you must rest. Sleep now and the God of many names be with you.' He turned to go.

'Wait, wait.' Dare she? But she really wanted to know.

'How old are you?' she blurted out.

'Older than you,' he said, 'and yet young enough.'

With that, on an instant's breath, fast-slow as a gnat's wing, Yahwiel had gone.

Chapter 6 Dreams , hell, and not-dreams

Well it was true it *had* been a bit exhausting. Maybe a short rest. She'd just shut her eyes for a moment.

But first she knew she had to go down that steep winding staircase. Iron. Quite attractive to look at. But unending to clamber down.

And it would be further down still. She knew. Agony.

She knew it was to hell. Her own fault. Her own hell. Hadn't her mother told her that when she'd clambered up the step ladder to get the jam on the top shelf? Or hidden the torch-lit book under her pillow? None so bad as what she had now ...

Stop! How go further? But she knew she had to, they were waiting down there for her. Chris and Holly that she'd betrayed (*don't think about that. FORGET!*).

Oh there, like Aladdin: the trapdoor in the corner, how heavy the heaving heave of the ring, more stairs, heaves, down, heaves, down down downest.

A heavy door. She must pound on it pound pound pound, batter it down. Chris was in there calling for her and Holly too and unless she could get to them they'd be devoured by the gruesome dragon that was just about to shake the door down. Chris was shouting. Holly was barking, Kate was shaking, the dragon was coming ...

Yes Kate was shaking. Shaking herself awake. And there she lay on the deck of Pearl of the Seas. In the bright sun. And Holly was barking frantically and trying to push with her nose and Chris had closed himself down below by mistake and was pounding pounding to be let out and only Kate could open the hatch for him..

So she did. Oh!!

So on they sailed through sunlit seas and dawns and the winds' songs and Holly's leaps. And the blackness of the sea at midnight.

So here are rheir thoughts, voyagers' thoughts,

Here not the land, firm land, alone appears, may then by them be said,

The sky o'erarches here, we feel the undulating deck beneath our feet,

We feel the long pulsation, ebb and flow of endless motion,

The tones of unseen mystery, the vague and vast suggestions of the

briny world, the liquid-flowing syllables,

The perfume, the faint creaking of the cordage, the melancholy rhythm,

The boundless vista and the horizon far and dim are all here.

This is ocean's poem.

Chapter 7 The sea and the sky

And the ship whispered to Chris of it hidden ways, for she trusted him b=now, and taught him her secrets. And he sang to her tuning and carried her in his thought and dream through the wine dark sea and the foam of the waves. No small boy now, but the Skilled Skipper who understood the melody of his ship, the Hero cleaving the ocean, steering to the eastern far of his dream.

And many monsters they met there. But the Hero drove his ship fast through them. And when the weeds clung and hung and stung from the deepest bed of the ocean, hard, when they threatened his ship he slashed her way through them with his knife.

And Kate admired him from where she sat at watch amidships, and Holly proud on the prow. For they knew that they were his crew, his team.

So then they came to the wandering blue rocks, those Kate had dreamed of once.

They saw them first in the distance, coming fast toward them (*or were they coming ones? who knows in this Einstein age?*), they saw them shining like spires and castles of bright glass, while an ice-cold wind blew from them and chilled their hearts. Even Holly's .

And they neared them. Heaving rocks, as they rolled upon the long sea-waves, crashing and grinding together, till the roar went up to heaven. Any days and years they sailed. The sea sprang up in spouts between them, and swept round them in white sheets of foam; but their heads swung nodding high in air, while the wind whistled shrill among the crags.

But Man of Action had pulled down the sails. 'Between these rocks we must pass; look for an opening, and be brave.'

Then he stood and watched. Quiet quiet quiet as the best men of action are.

'Don't know' - now where had she ...

A heron, a heron was what she needed. A *heron*?

'No herons in the middle of the sea' aid Chris. Even more shortly, surely he must be right?

But Kate breathed and breathed. And sang:

Do not be afraid bright heron heroning,
to-stand to wait and wade
by the waters motionless.
And then – a flash A gleam - !
To spear your trout
and then
to take us through ...

And lo, a heron grew into her song, a feathered waiting shape and there it was before her eyes.

And before all their eyes.

For they saw a heron come flying mast-high toward the rocks, and hover before them. It was looking for a passage through.

But - 'Our ship isn't a *bird*,' said Chris shortly, 's pearl, surely you know that.'

'Oh I don't know,' said Kate. Dashed (*but wasn't dashing just the thing, dashing and clashing and gnadhing like the rocks and washing-in-the sea and ... and ...*).

And so they watched again.

The heron waited, waited, waited. And the right moment, the very nick and notch and nudge of time, it spread its heavy wings. And it creaked high into the air, ponderous, pondering, looking at the rocks' movement. Like a trout moving in the stream where it watched. And like an arrow - it *flew!*

And the blue rocks clashed together as the bird fled swiftly through. And showed the way. The rocks had lashed and hit and bit and rebounded back without hurt to the bird.

'A pilot! follow the bird,' shouted Kate.

So Chris and Kate shouted, and Holly barked, and all three manned the oars (*well Holly was supposed to dog them, to push and pull with her rump and all her might - not the best way, but there you are, we all love dogs*).

But Holly – when she saw Kate looking at her she leapt instead, all huff and pride, to the very mast top; and stood surveying the sea and the rocks and her subnets below. Prided of place indeed. Her tail high, highest of all things of that great ship, as a pennant flighting proud and flagsome to the sky (*beautiful it was too, beautiful I tell you. like a bird, like that heron flying*).

Pride, pride must have its fall you say? You are wrong. She fell not. Sure footed. But look - there she was rejoicing and barking and crying out in her doggie way 'We're through, bow, bow wow wow' - and the rocks clashed together with a fine bang, the toppest crags of them, the clanging lastest. And they had caught - oh caught the tip of Holly's tail. That's why dear children, why Holly and all the dogs like her, have only half a tail. One side proud, whirling, upright. the other - well, *nothing!* Or maybe only magic dogs.

Not that Holly knew. She thought she was still there, all fine, prow head masthead twirling her pride before her, sorry behind her.

And so she was and is till the end of time. Holly! Tail up. Proud. But, ssssh, only half a tail. Dear Holly.

But concentrate, back to the proper tale (*not 'tail', you sillies out there!*). And the two were rowing now. *Get away!* The oars bent like withies beneath their strokes as they rushed between those toppling ice-crags and the cold blue lips of death. And before the rocks could meet again they had passed them, they were safe in the open sea.

So they sail-ed on, a-safened now, in a fine breeze. And all was well again. So on again they went through the dark water and moonlit starred nights. A long way round the world, had Chris not known? But all indeed would be well.

She was adrift. Kate. Alone. Baked in the sun dried in the wind parched in the thirstiness. On a raft. Just the great sea, the sky, the sun the sun the sun. Burning.

They had forgotten her. Sailed on. Away. Even Holly, dear Holly, even Holly.

Was that a bark across the sea? No just the seagull calling. The horrible seagulls.

Kate closed her eyes. Might as well die now.

Oh then her dream - ship in distance, sailing away. Ship in distance, sails down. Head in water. Chris. Swimming. Pulled up on raft.

Ship still sailing. Sky sun above.. But ship ship gone, Chris *Chris!!* look ship gone.

But no - long rope snaking through sea under sea, over sea. To ship to safety. Chris pulling them to ship, rope starting to fray.

Ahh, soft touch on her cheek, moisture, wetness she never thought to feel again.

It was Holly's moist tongue that was licking her. There, lying on deck. Aah.

Sea gulls calling in the sky.

'A bad dream Kate?' asked the skipper, 'I heard you calling ... ?'

Aah - a dream, just a dream *(but in this world are they 'just' dreams?)*

Lovely seagulls in the sky.

And so they sailed on in peace. She the dreamer *(but was it? what is dream, what reality, what the utterly voyage of our lives?)*. He the Hero. Holly the Holly. For many days. Across the globe.

A-sudden. Ship heeled-over. More again and m-o-ore. So slowly ...

They were sinking. And see an awful sea-full dreading-full gash in her side. that very gash and dash and CRASH, cracking her side, as the ship left its first harbour, in that abandonment by Kate so long ago. And look the gash was growing and grown, it filled the ship, the sea, the sky. *Kate's* hole, Kate's hole-filled guilt-filled fault. The gash - fault in the rock, i' the hold, the unholding hold 'gainst the sea.

Oh what to do? Huge but in awkward narrow place, you cannot reach it. It was for Kate to mend, to darn. She *had* to. And into her mind came that fleeing dreams, its shreds, flighting past, could she catch them. Yes!

'I dream-ed once,' she falteringly began, ' - I was in in hell. And, and the dam was holed. To plug. I must I must. so then they told me (who? oh there are countless names, I cannot count, you know that sure) they told me shudder-task, to cut my finger.Off. I could not do it. *Could not.* Pain. And terror. Fear. But had to.'

Holly looked up and reached a paw. Then looked at Kate and went below.

And look, just look, *her* paw could reach where no man went before. And plugged and filled. And the gap grew small and covered itself. And Kate reached down and did the darn. 'So that will do for now,' she said. Schooling come into its own (*we told you so, we did*). And all was well again.

And what did Holly find when she was scrabbling down there below? Yes. *Ginger* beer. I tell you, some tales end good!

So they sailed on. And on. Eastward all eastward. For round the globe.

But Holly, oh so pleased with herself got careless. Ohh! there she goes! Overboard again. *Again.* Just two little paws scrabbling to hold onto the gunwale. Maybe she deserves it but, well, Holly!

In dives the Skipper, Man of Action he! Kate trembling hands on tiller, stand-in, do best, oh come back Chris, come back. Even *without* Holly. How dare you leave me!

Oh *yes!* Chris! Well done, Chris. Well done well done, pull you up. Boathook, rushed below, get't, tangled legs coming up ladder, oh forgotten what it's called on a ship stop muddling up, Holly can dry in sun, so drenched and salty.

'Oh don't be so cross Chris, I *had* to leave tiller to look. And pull you in. Yes all right yawing and floundering and whatever the jargon is. Well all right but who cares, land miles away. Oh all *right* then, *you* take over. *I* don't care. '

'Next time *leave* her? You mean that Kate?'

'*Yes.* Ah, no. Oh don't care, going below ... '

Off she stumped. Fell over boathook all over again, right down stairs. Thump thump. Well, maybe she did care. A little. Kate hugged Holly, big sobby hug, and buried her head in her fur, didn't make any difference that it was wet.

So that was the second time of saving *(why tell us that? aha, just wait).*

Ah, sight of land. At last at last. But - what was that? a song. A *song*? A melody of lovely-ing bending blending wending sending vocalising voices. In the breeze. A beautifullest sweetest song. Time to sleep *(Kate was good at that. We know!).* Even the Great Man of Action at the tiller harkened. And drooped a bit. And Holly yelped out in her dreams. No not a nightmare. A sweet song sweet I tell you.

All things stayed silent. Harkening. The gulls sat in white lines along the rocks; on the beach great seals lay basking and kept time with lazy heads; while silver shoals of fish came up to hearken, and whispered as they broke the shining calm. The wind overhead hushed his whistling, as he shepherded his clouds toward the west; and the clouds stood in mid blue, and listened dreaming, like a flock of golden sheep.

And the heads of our three heroes drooped, even Holly's. They closed their eyes and dreamed of bright still gardens and murmuring pines, till all their toil seemed foolishness, and they thought of world-rounding then no more.

But Kate, Kate, the one who could not sing, still again she woke and sang. To preserve her dear loves her friends. She sang. Her song was quiet quiet and more quiet than the world, but yet the winds heard, the still air, the ship too.

"Life is short, but life is sweet;
and even men of brass and fire must die.
The brass must rust, the fire must cool,
for time gnaws all things in their turn.

Life is short, but life is sweet:
and joy, and a bounding heart, to earn
a landfall sweet."

And Kate's quiet voice rose like a flute through the evening air and echoed like a bell through the skies till the rocks rang and the sea; and it rushed like wine into their souls (*sorry, like ginger ale*). So that it drowned the enticing voicing vicing melody from the jagged tempting wrecking shore. And they rowed on.

And presently they set the sails again for the wind was fair. And they thought that now the worst was gone, round the world soon to be accomplish-ed, and they could return and tell it to their parents in their own dear land.

Little they knew! As they lay a-resting after their ordeals, what happened? The clouds were gathering, stirring up from the sea the rage of every wind that blows till earth, sea, and sky were hidden in cloud. And it was black night.

Winds from East, South, North, and West fell upon them all at the same time, and a tremendous sea got up.

And it broke over the Pearl with such terrific fury that she reeled again, and even the Man of Action was forced to let go the helm. The hurricane was so great that it broke the mast half way up, and both sail and yard went over into the sea and the ship was covered with water. You no longer saw her held in Kate's breathing under the ocean's surface.

And then, look, her mast appearing, little little little on the surface then her deck - but oh tossed all about. Think how the winds of autumn whirl thistledown round and round upon a road. Yes, like that. The winds were playing battledore and shuttlecock with her, all at once. Then a terrible great wave reared itself up up and up, and more up as Kate held her breath (*and all the world too I think, me at least - up, up, UP ...*) above their heads till it broke right over the ship which shuddered like a heap of dry chaff tossed about by a whirlwind, death staring in their face.

But when the third day broke, the wind fell and there was a dead calm without so much as a breath of air stirring. and that was hard too. But they would row. Once they knew the direction. *And* they would get Holly to help, *whatever* she said - er, barked.

And Kate's memories-map (*school some use, see?*) showed them the way. And that was good. And her numbering - not so good. Directioning even worse. *Map* okay but - but wrong way up! Oh Kate Kate! (*Fancy dancing prancing trusting Kate's way-uppingness, not her thing at all at all!*). But still. Nearing land perhaps? S*omeone's* land anyway. Kate on the lookout. Insisted. Mast top.

Scary at first. But then - the calm sea. Clear air. Heavens above her. So she sang quietly to herself she the no-singer (*no one listening by then, thank the lord - if there was a lord ... Many names once you're at sea*). She was remembering the perils of the deep from which something, someone, strong to save, had saved them. It was a prayer. of thanks and peace. Kind-of

I long for land as one

by hurricane oppressed
lost in the storm-crossed ocean
by storm and wind distress't
goes without rudder sail-less
no friend no love in sight -
O look from the mast-top sailor
look past the ocean's sight,
look for the harbour's shelter
and give me lastly ...

'Land!' shrieked Kate, 'ho! land there! I see it. Ho!' (*she knew 'ho' meant land in some language or other, 'Westward ho', that was it wasn't it ...)* I see it, landwestwardho, ho west, look look, ' she cried pointing wildly to the east (*oh oh Kate, directions? Squew-whiffy. Very*). Well that was all right, east let it be.

But oh Kate, why point? Let go? Lose your un-footing. Tumble whirl skirl fall maul, flapping hair tumbling eyes open shutting fear what now terror hell? Whence there is no return.

And so she *fell*. Into that watery grave. Whence no return? Ship departing, fierce wind behind.

Alone in the sea, with the sky.

Worse than the raft, there at least she wasn't cold.

Seagulls.

Never more alone.

Chris twisted the tiller, man of action by now he was (*had to be*), struggled, fought. Ship so slow, fight again. Around. Against the wind. Beat. (*mast mended? Yes, magic times you know*).

But where? oh WHERE?

Kate gone so soon.. Lost. Mighty waves. HUGE HORRIBLE WAVES, curling and furling, spiteful. Mightful. Engulfing Kate.

No crew.

Worse - NO KATE. And - and - well she was only a girlie, but he did quite I- like her. Quite (*keep cool now. Distance rightest for skippers – but oh oh ... And her mum*).

And - oh but where is Holly? Oh Gone. GONE. Overboard?

No oh oh no look look!

Little head above waves. Just behind ship. Oh and they'd got back to her, there she was all the time. Kate. Drowning? No swimming. On her back. Loving the sky, the clouds, not wanting to .... Dreaming. Stay asleep

Oh Holly was licking her face, waking her, waking her. No mistaking. Holy Holly.

'Bring her in,' yelled Chris (man of action) twisting the tiller again, commanding the sails to drop (skipper!). Rope. Throw. Action!

And Holly little Holly was putting her little arms (*legs you duffer -no, but she was almost human now, saviour*) round Kate's neck. And Kate put her arms right back round *her* neck. And saw the rope. And threaded it through Holly's unbreakable (*well we will see*) collar. And the man of action hauled and hauled and pulled them right right up onto the deck. And collapsed them there.

He collapsed himself too (*men of action fragile, very, my mother says*).

And then what a crying and a sighing there was. All round. All but Holly. She just wanted her supper. And the ship sailed on. East..

Kate cried out from her mast head, cry-ed out. aloud. 'Make for land, Chris, make for land.' Chris, carpenter-son, knew better. What more dangerfull for ships, small, large, any in th' universe, than jagged shores. Tsunami-cast ships up. Up to the violent feuding volcane-tops with molten lava down and down to deeps and fire below and everlasting hell again ...

Best run the ocean wave howsoe'er the winds. And so he did. The Skipper.(*ignore the witless wetting fearful crew, know-nothing them*).

But no! Fate not allow. Surf up and up against the rocks thundering as the swell burst against them'gain and yet again.. Everything enveloped in spray. No harbour for a ship to ride, no shelter. Just the jutting headlands, low-lie rocks and rocks and rocks, and mountain tops.

The wind was driving them onto the rocks. and rocks, and rock again. And rocking ship. And winds a-rock as well.

Breathe breathe Kate. What use of inspire-ationing if not the breath of life of calm of gentle wind.

She tried. She did.

And the wind fell calm and sweet and brought them soft onto the sandy shore. a shore of paradise it truly was.

Well that's what Kate had intended. Her story. Her dream. Her life.

The wind might have died. But the waves. From beyond the horizon seen. Still hashing, lashing, dashing crashing,, boiling curling above and between between between. All those rocks and - oh careful (*scream*), on left, on port I mean, starboard larboard (*where's that?*). Oh *everywhere*.

But Chris skilled skipper, man of action brave was at the helm, his own-made tiller, jewel precious as the stars,, as the phases of the moon it was to him. His own-make, first.

He held it soft in his hand, steered through the waves. Now port now starboard, now alongside curling furling waves high above, no inning, getting small, just ord' waves now, just wavelets, ripples. Aah. Release and breathe again.

But oh that unseen, unforeseen point-jag, just there, just there. Ship safe indeed, roll gently, side on side , oh safe, ashore, no not ashore, just lapping wavelets by the sand, adrift, a-side, along, relieve, release, of real. Of peace.

But - the tiller. The Skipper's own outward homeward tiller, for safe over boiling sea in his maker's saving hands. It was gone. Smashed to - worse than smithereens.

Beyond repair.

Chris yelled at Kate, in fury uncontrolled and bursting out.

'You *fool*, you brought us here, didn't stop the singing stupid songs they didn't work. and numbering unnumb'ring countless numeration yours.   Gone. Oh my own my own, my ship, my Pearl, never to sail again, oh my own my helm, nevermore 'n my hand. For guidance. Oh my life, nevermore to breathe.'

And he, the Man of Action now no longer now, he hard, he dear friend Chris, he burst int' tears, bowing his head over the shattered dead wood that had smiled for him, live like a bird. Over the seas. To round the globe. And *that* gone now too. Too desolationing.

Tears of anger? Yes. But more - despair, a life end.

Kate went to him, tried to put arms of comfort round her dearest friend. Comrade grown from small boy once to now wise skipper, master of the sea. Now again a little, lost, boy. Dear Chris!

The Hero of Heroes? Well, but he was ... nothing.

Mast gone too. Did you not see? What ship, be she ever so a pearl, e'er flighted through the seas without a mast.

So as the hoar frost goes from the grass when the sun brightens its rays

- as the song of the dawn birds disappears int' the sky and is gone

- the songs of angels echo unheard in the skies when men are born

even so vanish-ed the light from the eyes of the Great Skipper, never to return (*oh but it was it was? was that the story we were told? wait wait my children dear*).

Kate tried to catch it as it fell. But who can catch the light, the wind? Who see it? And now it had turned, it was just - tears. Tears soaked in the ground. Gone.

He wasn't Hero now. Oh just her friend. Her pal. So many undergone adventures. So many savings of her dog. Could she not comfort him?

She laid her hand gently, so gently, gently, on his arm.

He threw her off in fury. Furiously!

'Could we not mend ...?? ' So timidly. So fearful of that black anger, thundercloud, hurr'cane, tsunami all. Engulfing. Even her.

He punched her. *Punched* Kate*! Furi-ous* and *furiouser* and ....

'Or - another? Look lots of trees and ...'

'And where do you think we'll find an awl you fool? or saw? in this something something something hellish witchiest island? *You.* And knife's bcount too. Oh *girls*! ' (*that fair d'you think?)*

'Maybe - get help?'

'Don't be so *stupid*! In a *desert* island! *You!,* and out he hit at her again the lout (*don't* worry, *he loved her really, best pal ever, just he was very cross, well - agony - men feel it worst you know*).

Holly dogged quick out of his way. More sensible than Kate for she was still trying, crying.

Kate, even more timidly, 'Should we maybe tie her up? Just in case? another storm might ...'

'Don't be so silly.'

Holly frolicking (*frolicking!!*) up the shore. And back.

Footprinting, foursome-ing and dogsome-ing.

And lo, the footprints are filling out, enlarge-ening. They are, they are - links in a chain. A long one. Steel, strong, light, shipwise flexening.

Chris picked the chain from the ground, from the sand, and made his ship fast to a tall tree. No moving now (*no moving ever ...*).

Then he sat on the ground and wept. And looked at the wreck. Wreck of hopes, of life, of lifelong storyfull hopes.

Chris, no longer now the Man of Action, past dreams more like. He look-ed up, despair at the hard relenting-less troubling tussling clouds. And then ...

A great city. And men, or was it men 'n' lions, walking its streets. Great palaces and yes yes a joinery. Wood, planks*, joists,* a-heaped outside.

'Kate look, *not* uninhabited, how could you have thought that? ' (*hm*) 'Look? Yes, awls, timber, saws ...'

Mirage, of course. That wasn't Chris. Imagination not his thing. A dream? (*but what is dream?*) a hope?

But good thought Kate ... Now they could go to find that help they sought. For ship, even for themselves. Just (*ssh*) like she'd said in the first place!

Chris started up the shore towards the trees. (Paradise did I say? The happy end? Not no, of thorns. And trials still. Just wait).

Kate tried and died to follow, for well she knew if not with them she would be lost.. But her head ached so, her knees, her limbs, her very self (" *... as easy from myself I might depart.*"). She could not.

He was gone.

The end.

And Holly with him too.

Alone.

The end.

Chapter 9 Thorns in paradise

But look, look there! Flicker of a tail. A half tail. Holly.

And oh Kate *could* run, had to. Holly gone again but fast after her ran Kate. Impenetrable thicket, thorns. No help for it, had to go.

Track through the broken branches, little silver hairs caught on a thorn, the shreds, the smell of Chris' ire hanging in the air.

Easy to follow. But hard the way, and harder. Struggle struggle.

Blister on her heel, but no time to stop. Felt - what - a blessed plaster in pocket, just one, oh dearest mother mine.

'Chris Chris wait for me, oh wait wait, while I put ... ' No she was *not* going to cry. Can't stop for that.

Nothing to do but struggle on.

Heel blister now rubbed raw. No chance to stop, would lose them sure.

Had she lost ... ? Panic. Oh, now, there was a sign from Holly's print. Relief.

Breathe Kate, oh breathe.

And struggle on.

Ah, within sight.They'd stopped. Looked round. Chris taking off shoe.

'Think blister just starting. Under big toe. Ouch.'

'Oh oh here Chris, I have plaster, it'll help.'

Takes it. Puts on. No thanks.

Off again but now she was closer. In sight. A little easier. Limping now, and Holly too.

He'd stopped again. His shoe slipped off (*no longer hero, no nor skipper now, just - small boy, afraid in undergrowth*).

'Oh Chris, let me fasten it for you with - yes, the ribbon from my plait, look here!'

And so it was.

Kate's hair unbound, catching in thorn trees as she bent under. Not mattering the pain, too much else in her mind. And when Holly's unbreakable collar broke off, what but the other ribbon. More catching snatching watching gnarling thorns in hair, little she cared. for she was following after still, that all her mind was on.

He'd stopped. Berries on thorn tree, thirsty now. He tried one, cut it with his knife, then knife on ground (forgot!).

Holly smelled them . No no, not not for her.

For Kate, oh solace for her thirst, at last. But had he left her any? No! No chance! No not one. or one swift glance back.

Now what? Edge of the great domain. Thick thicker thickest thicket-hedge. High ladder over..

How to mount? Chris, not easy, hoisted Holly to the top. Then jumped and jumped for the first rung. Held on. Just. Pulled up. Yes, he was there. Climbed up to platform at the top. No look back still.

Dis'peared and thump bang landed t'other side, and Holly after, easy. Disappeared and gone.

And Kate?

Too high, too lone too lost too left behind.

Again.

She was happy for them really. For *them*.

But for her?

As the lone thistledown falls solitary down and fails to seed

- as the falling star misses its fine target on the earth

- as the blown spume fails to meet again the wave it's left

even so was Kate.

Alone. Unliving, unexistent, failed. Alone and lost in the wild wood. And no way back. Abandonment.

In its nine circles, cycles and recycles of her being, her own. In the dust, the dirt, the desolation that was the *worst* could ever ever fall to man in all the centuries of the great world's being.

They had forgotten her.

Slowly slowly, oh so slowly, lifetime's beat of a mosquito's wing, a caterpillar changed to wonder-of-the-world, she look-ed down and down and down, down into her heart. Agony to overwhelm the typhoon pain. Agony she had never known before.

Forgotten her.

It was true. No retreat now into dream, dementia or amnesia. Those blessed states. He had *forgotten* her. Her exist –, but she did not, now, exist.

Her echoed shriek unsounded silent (all the worse), her shriek to the four blown quarters of the universe, and back and back, back, back, reflected in her heart, and shimmered, shattered, swingen shut, bells from ruined churches, falling stars, and broken chords, cadences unresolved ... hers now *not* hers, but not exist, could not be hers.

She tried to sing, but no help there. Try all the same:

I wasn't needed.
I heard the angel song,
music of man's desire.
I was not there.
I was not wanted.
The sweet land's king sure wanted me.
But wasn't looking when I came.

I stood behind the hedge. Alone.
So de-sole-ate. I was not needed there.
My friends were there, forgetting me.
I was right glad for them.
They had forgotten me.
Silence.

But not sweet music's silence, the muses' poet-words. Not silence of dear assonance of scansion sweet performancing. Or breeze caressing trees.

Dead silence, deaf and negative. Empty like noise, like din.

Just silence there. No sound.

Silence.

Chapter 10 King Aahal of The Many Names tells the Great Tale of Language

And Chris? Confused he was, near overcome with sleep and drowsy-ness. And there was something, something to remember, something awful done or not done. Where ...? Oh and his quest. His life work. Given up. And his *own* choice. Fatal mistake. and something else was there too ...

But now he found himself before a king. And Holly too. A queen there too?

The king was speaking now, must gather self. A-telling of the land's own yth and why he welcome was, from it.

'Once upon a time,' he began, 'all creatures if the earth understood one another. They had their own languages, it us true, and ways. But they understood. But ine day, I do not know why, perhaps it was through some strange being call-ed Sinner, we do not understand when or wherefore, they gathered all together under some great tree (some say it was a high building but that I do not believe), and there in the pride and foolishness of their hearts, they climbed it. And those on each branch, the great branched Tree of Language, high, were speaking now each a new tongue. And the great understanding between creatures was gone as if it had never been. Of dogs and lions only understanding still.

Alas that act was the very disaster of our world. We live with it still. Only the dogs it was that refused to climb. They said they did not like heights. The others laughed and jeered. But they stood firm. They lay quiet quiet at the foot of the tree, them only we understand and speak with now.

At that the queen and Holly looked at each other, Holly with one foot raised where a thorn had deep-pierced her soft paw.

' And then came the time,' went on the king, ' but it is still to come, for what is time, when a young boy cane from the west, from the far mage Country of Myth and Mist. You will know him they said by the hero light about his head. .And with him came a creature walking soft and hard upon three legs' (Holly lifted her head, sleepy but interested).

' I think it was a dragon for on its back, tail-like, dragon way, was a fiery plume, bright, flaming, on the one side red as blood, on the other black as smoke, vanishing in the air.

Then,', his voice grew hushed, ' on the fiftieth day came a great magician and singer, man or woman we know not, but in human form. .And that great magician put rout to Saint Sinne. And lo we spoke still in our many tongues, but at last with understanding each of each, throughout all the land. And the lion lay down and spoke gently with the lamb'.

'My dear,' said the queen reproachfully but with affection too, 'thus we have heard so often. He too,' nodding at Chris who was still standing there feeling very confused, ' perhaps. But do you not see she is in pain. Dear Holly' (*how did she know her name?*) 'come here my poor dear.'

And tenderly, gently, with great care she drew out the thorn. And wiped the place with the end of her garment. And long the two spoke together of secrets that were to come, and looked in each other's eyes.

'Come then my son" said the king, ignoring, back to business he, ' and welcome here. My greetings and those of my land. But me ask you of your name and your way here. For I am the king of this country whom they call The King of Many Names, and here too is my Queen, Iram. I greet too your dear companion Holly, dog of many skills, frisking now with my reddest setter Olud, four legs again, now together eight.

'Your name? Your journey? How came you to the Land-Where-No-Man-from-the-West-has-Yet-Visited, the No Where Land?'

'I am Chris,' he started, wanting to be Hero, 'small boy from the west, and I came here with ... '

'You were so brave, you and Holly,' said the queen, 'just the two of you.'

'Oh. NO!!' shouted Chris . And the leth-e-forget-berry scales fell swift and hard from his eyes, 'No no no. KATE!!! WHAT HAVE YOU DONE WITH HER?' Just now she was here. WHERE? Hidden? Not - not *dead*?'

And he hid his face in his hands. Worse than the ship. Worse even than the no-world-round. It came in a rush, a gush, gash, slash of emotion ... No impossible, that ladder, that jump and fall. That that - that utterest sin. His dear comrade, her, his friend-in-arms. His Kate. Abandonment.

'*That's* all right then,' said the queen, looking across at the king. 'At the Great Ladder-Way you say?'

'Don't worry,' said the king,' the lions'll have found her.'

'*What*. - No oh *NO !!'*

The queen, not understanding, tries to allay.

'It's all right stranger, they love children for their cubs to play, to teach them new.'

Chris – still fearful. *Horrified*. Ashamed. How can he get back to her? Ladder t'other side of hedge too high for him to jump. No way. For no one can. He howls with fear and misery.

But see musician there. Same name, or near-enough, was Krishinan. So Krish (for short) he overheard Chris's howling noise. Thought it was heavy metallic sound aha, was rocking, musicking (*mistake*), so took to him.

Hey fella, here!' all quiet-like (a rock-gig-guy *quiet! but 'twas needed* f'them) 'Look hole in hedge. I made it there, a secret exit, don't ask why. If go out there and round the back, you'll get there fine. Go quick afore they sees.'

So spoke he and Chris heard. And went. Small boy. Afraid. But hardened heart and went.

So off went Chris. A little hero-ed p'raps this time, but still ashamed (*quite right)*. And Holly, not a-shamed, not one bit 'shamed,, leapt off the queen's knee (yes, titbits left, red setter too - just backward glance 'neath eyelashes) and followed, uninvited. What dog refuses expeditioning and walkies? *Smellies too*. Faithful as well of course, an after-thought (she thinks - but we know better. Dearest Holly).

So Chris took many hours through thorns, a-trudge. He faithful too I think. And Holly close behind. Curse her for tagging on, long tangled hair in thickets caught, again again, come back and back and holding up from reaching Kate (*oh Kate oh Kate, by lions got? eaten not play?*), but no way, panting fainting, he can abandon Holly, Holly of Kate's (*oh Kate ph Kate*).

Try run try run. Oh walk, oh marching song to help No can, no breath ... Oh Holly front, keep up keep up oh can't oh breathe. Oh Holly ...

What? She's smelling, Scent the air. Oh!

KATE!

Oh happy end.

Chapter 11 *Of Kate and King and the knowing of not knowing*

But Kate - she wasn't going to play *that* game.

Have been abandoned, then say happy every after?

No! she was *seriously* annoyed - to have been left behind. Forgotten there! She turned her back with a hard stamp (*ouch, the blister, still not cured; and sore ...*). An'way no way to get her over th'impossible impassable ladder. Oh (*sob*) unsurmountable, *why* did they have to do it like that-a-way. Useless story. No way up.

'Back the way I came?' suggested Chris - and *he* was timid now.

'And I 'spose you know the way back huh?'

'Well er, yes, well no, well - .'

But Holly dear Holly came and put her head so gentlewise right on Kate's knee. And looked her thoughts. A dog remembers. And can *smell.* And find the way.

So all was well. For Holly led and that was good.

But - 'ware the rising tide, escaped till then. And storm. Cut off. Not back not on. But drowning soon. Stopped by a chasm over the foaming sea, The rising rising tide, moon led, the spring, the worst Oh what to do?

Holly tried first , brave dog, to jump across. But down she slipped and fell right in. Oh down goes Chris (*third time*) and pulled her up. Then toppled, toppled, nearly in.

But Holly - had he not three times saved her, himself?

See Holly's magic now, magic transformationing. A lovely marble bridge, high over the flooding sea.

But Kate is still afraid. What if she fell? the bridge's too narrow, slippery, no not for her But Chris's arms are there, they're rails to shield her, gold and silver-made.

So then? So then Kate walked across, and Chris and Holly, true shapes again, walked after. Walked into that fair land.

And fair it was. The rivers ran with lemonade. Under the tree roots lay hid coffee ('xcept Holly got there first, 'twas only natural). Musicking, rock and all, that scented the air.

Even better, everyone loved them The lionesses even loved Holly. Envious but still they loved her. and the queen adored her.

But best of all, for Kate, was the Unknowing-Knowledge of the king. He

the moon. The universe. And then, most sacred of them all, of the creation.

'A poem perhaps? Was it perhaps, perhaps,' Kate hesitated, it seemed, well, *too* miracle-like, 'like when a bird lays its first eggs and almost not believing shows them to her ... Shy.'

'Yes,' said the King, 'yes, like that.'

And he shut his eyes, remembering and marvelling:

As the blackbird shows

first to her mate
heart burst of pride and joy
her heav'n-song:
blue as the sky
from whence they came
as sea wherein they rolled
of th' eyes of the one you love
with whom you breathe

So the creator too showed
in his first create
the earth for man
his heartburst joy
breath'd wond'rous love
his worldes whole
of bird and plant
and most of all
for earth he made
(what greater love has any man?)
his creatures all
of humankind.

'Yes', said Kate ', breathing deep, like in my favourite hymn, well nearly, like:

God be in my mind
and in my sinning
God be in my womb

and my beginning

God be near to me

today, tomorrows

for time for life

for joy and sorrow

So God be with me there

when soul is flying

when mother's care ca-an reach

when lives are dying.

'The pearl within the pearl, ' murmured the king to himself, 'Yes that, just like that.'

Kate looked puzzled. Very. 'That sounds like nonsense.' she said. 'Oh I suppose - is it poetry? Maybe that explains ... '

'You are right' said the king 'for the deep things it is poetry ...' (*'The sea,'* thought Kate). 'But the time is not yet. You will see ... '

All very odd she thought. He seemed to be getting all het up about - well nothing.

But she did have a great reverence for the king. So she put his words in her heart and now and them pondered them. Most of the time she just forgot all about it.

And than, another day.

'You think much of breath dear Kate. And that is good. But what, have you thought, what is it that you breathe?'

'Air I suppose,' said Kate, rather puzzled. 'Oh all right I give up, I don't know.'

'Not knowing, that is the beginning of wisdom.' said, the king sounding just like Yahwiel (looked quite like him, now that she thought about it, his way of thinking too, his mind).

'Ponder this well dear child. Think of the names of God you know. Or of my many names, are they not breaths?'

''Um,' said Kate.

Try 'Yahweh, the unsayable, *breathe* it. Yahhwehh. Yes? and Allhahh? Hallehluyhah. Hhholy. And all the rest.'

'Ye-e-s, 'said Kate, trying to breathe like that.

'As so. went on the king solemnly, 'every breath that living creatures breathe they breathe my names, the names of God.'

Well that was quite a thought to put in her heart. And Kate breathed and breached and breathed. Those many beautiful names of God that all creatures know, language or not.

What could Kate do to repay these great gifts?

'There is one thing,' said the king, hesitating at first (*not like him*) then getting stronger, ' the animals ...'

'I know I know,' cried Kate leaping to her feet in excitement, 'to teach them my language And learn theirs. And share our understanding.'

'That is it,' said the king.

And so it was. And Kate, the unnumerate, the un-singer, found she was a teacher. And the animals loved her. And she them.

There was *so* much to do and to think about.

'What is the truth?' asked Kate one day. 'I don't know ... oh, oh, maybe that's not so bad ... I once heard ... ' And she looked hopefully at the King of many names, remembering Yahwiel. Perhaps he was there too for his wise grey eyes seemed to be looking through the king' blue ones.

No, nor I,' said the king. ' But many centuries ago a great man wrote a missive to a small girl who had asked him who invented God. Listen to what he wrote'/ and he drew a much-read parchment from his breast, kissed it and read:

"Nobody invented me – but lots of people discovered me and were quite surprised.

They discovered me when they looked round at the world and thought it was really beautiful or really mysterious and wondered where it came from.

They discovered me when they were very very quiet on their own and felt a sort of peace and love they hadn't expected.

Then they invented ideas about me – some of them sensible and some of them not very sensible. From time to time I sent them some hints to help them get closer to what I'm really like.

But there was nothing and nobody around before me to invent me. Rather like somebody who writes a story in a book, I started making up the story of the world and eventually invented human beings like you who could ask me awkward questions!"

So they all loved it there, Holly too, cavorting round with - well, you can guess. All those titbits from the queen, she was getting to look quite round! Chris wasn't into the knowledge stuff and all that, quite young still really, but he liked the games, specially the leaf-tracerie-in-the-sky thing. Not competitive of course but you can't have everything. the lions were great to wrestle with too, and the leopards to run against. Wheee!

Chapter 12 Farewell

But one day after they had been there a year and day, the King called them all three to come to him.

'Time to go dear ones,' he said sadly 'you are needed there. From whence you came. In that land. By the dear ones who love you.'

They were horrified, Dumb. Well Kate was anyhow. Then into her mind floated the memory of her mum. And of Chris's dad. And a normal un-coffee-cakey teatime. Well, pancakes perhaps, as only here mum knew how to make them.

But even so they were stunned. Kate too.

Like as when those who die are sent back to live

- those who have reached heaven to suffer again on earth

- those who have shed they burdens in peace to lift them again

even like that, so did they hear his words with sorrow.

Well Kate did. She didn't mind about the ginger ale and all that. But she knew she had much to still learn. And, yes, even to teach. And how would the littlest lion cub with the lisp do without her help?

Chris actually rather liked the idea of getting back. Well he did until - oh! hadn't he failed in his undertaking. No round-world. And his dear ship scuttled and gone. And no mother when he got home either (though he loved his father indeed, much).

As a swallow wishes for his homecoming but doubts the crag for his nest

- as the falling star knows not his welcome on the earth, its where or whither

So Chris thought of his home, his mission unaccomplished, his father yet to find one who would care for his needs when himself was failing. It was hard.

'Yes I know, home, but but - ' started Chris in his confusion.

'I am sorry,' said the king sternly, 'it is decided. In three days you will be gone.' He spoke abruptly so they would not detect the sadness of his heart.

Holly said nothing. She wasn't attending.

'But I don't know what my mum will say', worried Kate, hanging her head. 'Missing all those teatimes. She must be at wits' end and I know, oh dear, she'll give me a huge scold. Perhaps – perhaps I shouldn't go back after all … '

'Don't worry' (*his favourite saying, wasn't it!*) said the King of All Names. 'I'll have a word with Yahwiel, he'll sort it. Eternity in an hour. dear Kate. You know it well. Or a wild flower. He'll make it a year ago.'

'*And* a day,' said Chris, a skipper needed exactness (*Kate hadn't noticed of course, not much of a calculator, was she?*).

'Yes of course young man,' said the king. 'You'll do all right you will. And you'll I find a surprise when you get there, you've earned it.'

'A nice surprise?' asked Kate in a trembling voice.

'*Very* nice.' said the king smiling.

'*And* you've both earned it,' added the queen happily. Very happily. 'All that loving work and friendship. And teaching the cubs to write'.

'What on earth can they mean?' whispered Kate to Chris. He tried to look blank but he had an inkling. Just an inkling. A hope.

And then came the time for present giving. How can you have farewelling without that? Even in the Land of Where-No-Where.

First Holly - a magnificent collar of rawhide and rubies to replace the one she had list from the king. From the queen a kiss and a special titbit (*you can guess which she liked best! Anyways the collar was HIDEOUSLY uncomfortable.*)

To Chris the queen gave a magical knife, super sharp, made by great Ogun king of all African smiths.

Then to Kate the queen gave a magic pearl, more beautiful than the sea.

Kate gazed at it, too wonder-struck to speak. At last she placed it in her shirt pocket.

'No no,' said the queen, 'you will lose it there. And yes,' her eyes became far-away 'you will indeed lose it but find it at the last. Your soul,'

All a bit puzzling, but to be obliging Kate stuffed it in her jeans pocket.

From the king, a harp (all right a guitar or a lyre or a whatever: same thing, all lovely.

'But I can't sing,' said Kate.

'No?' said the king.

So what could Kate do but sing? She took up the lyre and plucked its strings. Then:

> "*God be in my head, and in my understanding*
> *God be in my eyes and in my looking*
> *God be in my mouth, and in my speaking*
> *God be in my mind, and in my thinking*

God be at my end. And at our departing."

And all the listening lions wiped their paws surreptitiously across their face and in a might roar-chorus shouted out together their thanks to Kate, their teacher to talk them in their own language and hers too.

And Kate replied in *her* language. The language the lions understood. Thanks to her.

But back to the story. After that the climax. Surely. The farewell gift to the skipper, to him, to Chris, from the Mighty King of All Names.

The king looked Chris in the eye. Then he bent and picked a pebble from the ground in front of him. One pebble.

'Your gift my boy,' he said.

Chris bit his lip. Not that he *wanted* presents. But that they should love him so little. Given him - nothing. His heart sank within him. Those months of comradeship and loving and laughing. All to no purpose.

But Chris had been well brought up and said thank you nicely. He wanted to throw it down, but put it instead into his pocket. That pocket that he knew ended in a hole (*and in all that time, that long long time - well, it was too bad of Kate, she hadn't mended it had she - girls!!*). He knew that way he could 'just happen to lose it, oh dear! Oh. Must've been a hole in my pocket. Oh dear ... *So* sorry.'

No darner Kate, that indeed was true (*we knew that already did we not dear children, for all her brave attempts*). But the queen the queen herself, with her own hands had mended it. Perhaps she foresaw something? or it was destiny that flighty lightsome winsome frolicking lady taking a hand? Anyway the pebble stayed there safe till it was needed.

So, the Hero pocketed his disappointment - true heroism indeed - and at least he had the knife. He fingered it on his belt to check. No losing *that.*

Chapter 13 Return giving

And yes they were now indeed departing. With tears in all their eyes. Even the sore-heart hero-that-had-been.

Then he looked anxiously at Kate.

'But from us - we'd forgotten. You *have* organised farewell gifts from us, haven't you?' (girls responsible for that end of things of course).

'Course,' said Kate, ' I sang.'

'Oh that! A *song*'s not a gift,' said Chris, impatient to get to the *real* stuff. Manlike (*well not all. And after all he hadn't got a mum poor thing*).

'Not a *thing*. Like you can keep.'

'But it is,' said Kate, 'a song is for ever.'

'But they've given us - well you - *real* presents, (all right I know you can't count, don't want to more likely) - and anyway the singing wasn't from *me*. What can *I* ... ?'

'Yes,' whispered Kate, ' but how? I haven't even got a hair ribbon any more.'

'What happened to that? You *are* careless Kate!' Chris whispered back.

'Oh you, you - long story,' replied Kate.

She glanced at the queen who was looking preoccupied and a little sick. 'Sick with the sight of us I expect. I'd give my eyes to ... Oh well, maybe just being rid of us will be the best farewelling of all.'

She tried to sound convinced. But really she felt real bad about it. But (*you must have guessed*) Holly to the rescue. Just look at the pride and the love of her!

In she marched, Miss Holly proud, t=tail half erect, no, half-tail erect and - what? Five little balls of fluff tumbling after.

Tumbling, yes - but very *organised* tumbling (*that was Holly*). Two in front, one red one silver. Behind one silver, one red.

(The red setter at the King's feet looked away, embarrassed. But proud.)

And there, right there in the middle, trying hard to keep up and watched kindly by the brothers and sisters - the littlest of all, red silver both, wonder, all mixed together. Trying hard at tumbling like the others.

'O-o-oh,' breathed Kate, 'the beauties.'

Even Chris couldn't resist. 'Adorable,' and, 'so now we have our gifts to give. Bless you Holly.'

'But we can't, we *can't* separate her from her pups.' expostulated Kate. 'A mother ... '

'How about we take *one* home. For Holly to rear' - Chris the practical - 'give them four? Lets take home the littlest, the runt, always the favourite. The rest: one for the King; one for the queen; one for the Lion-King ... ' All the attendant lions heaved roar-sighs of approval. What fun they would have! Chasing the leaves and panting and painting the clouds (you've *seen it, haven't you, the evening sky)* and tumbling and jumbling and stumbling, and oh, whatever, fun, thanks be to Holly for ever and ever.

And then they all in a great roar-chorus again shouted out together their thanks to Kate, their teacher. And Kate replied in *her* language. The language the lions understood. Now. Thanks to her.

'But who will the fourth pup be for? difficult!'. Even Kate felt there was something missing in the count.

But at that moment Kate saw a swift look between the king and queen. And she *knew*. But didn't reveal.

'Holly.' she said, 'may we leave your littlest one?'

The king looked away embarrassed. And proud. What man wouldn't? But the queen smiled, and beckoned to Kate, What she said we do not know (*but we can guess*). Kate did not speak, for she was choking back a tear, whether of joy or sadness we do not yet know but she gave the queen a big big hug.

So now the time had really come for them to leave.

The king and the queen gave Holly one last pat and kissed Chris and Kate on both cheeks, and then once more again. Kate glowed. Chris wiped off the kiss when he thought no one was looking.

Their return was easier and quicker (*for so is it the way of life dear children*). The lions escorted them in a bunch, and the Lion-King himself carefully, gently, lovingly took the little pup softly in his mouth and with a smooth - oh so smooth for babies - put it on the topmost rung,

Then 'Up, up. Jump jump jumpety jump!' to the others. It was too far of course so the Lion-King gave a mighty mighty *mighty* heave and Kate was standing on the top. Another - and Chris. Holly jumped up, herself. She wasn't going entrust her little one to *anyone,* even Kate. She did think a little about the brood left behind, even a few tears (*you think dogs don't cry? shows how little you know*). But she knew they'd be all right and soon forgot, all those lovely *smells* to show her new pup.

So on they went.

And there on the way they found Holly's old collar on a thorn tree. They took off the rubied one and left it for the next comer (and was Holly glad of the exchange!). But they didn't notice the knife lying hidden on the ground.

And so they came, quick, to the shore of their disaster.

Not long now - how was it so hard when they came? - and they saw the ship. The bedgraggled ship, back broken, wings drooped, wings soaked in the wet.

And - still tied. Kate had been right. Chris had been right to heed her (*YES he had too!*) back then, in those old days before the fall.

'Chris,' whispered Kate timidly. 'Have you your gift? your pebble?'

'Course not, fell out o' me pocket hours ago. Well - '. Chris put his hand into his pocket. Slowly slowly he drew it out. There was the pebble gleaming clear in his hand, in all its dirt and majesty.

'It must have been there for a purpose,' whispered Kate. 'The King of Many Names always knows what he is doing.'

She went over to where the sad helm was lying. Broken. Dead. No more in the Great Skipper's hand to fly the sea.

'Look,' whispered Kate, 'it'll fit.'

She was looking at the empty socket in the very eye of the tiller, empty, useless.

'Try it, try it ... '

Chris took the pebble, small still stone-dead thing. Reluctantly. But Kate had been right about things before (*some* things) so he didn't like to say no. After all she had done.

He held the pebble to the light. Then to the tiller.

The hero light shone in his eyes.

And - it fitted it fitted it fitted. Like a glove, to an inch.

So

- as a needle eye looks to fit the thread pointed through by the sew-er's skill

- as the thrush' eggs fit her builded nest

- and a wise king to his subjects

so fitted the pearl to its socket

and to the tiller standing ready for its hero skipper's hand.

And its gleam mingled with the light in the Hero's eye and filled the sky, overcame the clouds, sang with the wind.

'The pearl,' said The Skipper, strong.

But a mast? What ship can fly without a mast?

And there in the very place where the hero's light, his tears, had fallen to the ground. And watered it. There had sprung a tree. High and lofty it was, arching to the skies, the moon, the sun, highest of the forest, swaying and proud, like a mast, with a bird singing from its topmost peak.

And as they looked the branches grew to sails billowing in the wind and the tall trunk was their mast.

And the ship was floating gently at the edge of the great ocean, held my its mooring.

'The Pearl of the Sea.'

Chris undid its chain. 'On board!' he cried.' And Holly and her pup and Kate embarked.

'Home!' cried Kate. And Holly nuzzled her pup in relief.

'Oh no,' said the skipper, 'Have you forgot. Our mission. Round the globe.'

Kate sighed. But what could she and Holly do. They were the crew.

So eastwards, ever eastwards, eastwards. And the winds were conspiring too and drove them steadily forward. To the east.

Chapter 14 The breath of breathing

But – but – a massive contrary-wending sea, right over the ship, burying the mast in its unstoppable might. Tempest-stirred hurricane, typhoon. A wind driving them backwards, no resisting, back back to the west.

The Skipper knew his skill. Swift swift and his ship swept safe behind a headland. Sheltered. No emergence till the wind dies or they will be carried will nilly to the – west. Chris's nightmare, the death of his mission. But for now = safe. Just to wait. As Kate once waited by the hedge. Patience only, and endurance..

But not safety for all. What is this? Holly swept into the sea by a colossal magic wave (*silly dog, why not cling on like Chris and Kate!*), And her pukp left yowling in despair, wobbling desperate to follow till caught and clutched

by Kate. Holly *in the sea.*!

'Leave her, leave her, do not abandon my dream', cries the hero's mind.

''Save her save her.' cries his heart.

Which?

(*I think dear children that you know…*)

He looks once at Kate. And plunges into the surging maelstrom. And survives.

How happy now Kate, Holly and the pup. They know the hero's heart is sore and say little. But every now and then they look at him, hearts swelling too full to speak.

And at the mast head sang the bird, rejoicing them on their way across the sea. Homewards under the steady hand and guidance of the Great Skipper, the Hero, the Man of All Actions.for if his heart trembled, his hand was sure.

And so they again sailed free under the sky. To the west, the west.

The boundless blue on every side expanding,
With whistling winds and music of the waves, the large imperious waves,
Or some lone bark buoy'd on the dense marine,
Where joyous full of faith, spreading white sails,
She cleaves the ether mid the sparkle and the foam of day, or
    many a star at night.

And so the ship flew on with the floating winds and wings through winding ways of the deep, and the ways of the moon's turnings.

And this time dear children - but I think you know - we see them fly to the sea's song and the wind's and the lyre plucked by Kate the singer.

This time no clanging rocks or voicing songs or sea monsters or frightsome fears.

So let us look again. Can you see them moving gently in to the very shore, the very daythey had left. But now. But so long ago.

And The Pearl of the Seas lay at rest in her own dear place.

Chapter 15 Next time?

The tide was full in, the evening just starting to come. Holly didn't wait. She jumped out into the water and rushed splashing ashore, then disappeared into the hills (*who was she meeting?*). Kate lingered a little looking round, tears a little in her eyes. Chris – wow, got quite courteous, waited and helped her ashore..

Chris and Kate climbed out and walked together to the water edge.

'That was good, wasn't it`/' said Kate.

'Brilliant, best ever. Only thing is, shame it's all over' responded Chris,

'But - gosh, why not another?'

'Build a new ship you mean, golly no, going through all *that* again'.

They looked back to their beautiful ship, standing clear and bright in the sunshine. But what - dissolving, dreamlike, misting, clouding: now they saw a log (was it their true vessel) floating gently in the water; that very log that so long ago, that morning, they had fashioned into a dragon of the seas.

And there, there in the sand, there before their eyes, was the very log from which they had so long before made their ship. And - it was the day they had left, nearly teatime

'Only a dream then ... ' despaired Kate.

'No,' said Chris strongly, 'just look here.' And he pointed to the seaweed stalks lying on the beach. What were they but the striking shape a tiller, the skipper's much-handled tiller? In its eye a single gleaming shell.

Kate felt in her pocket. The pearl. And the light of the two, pearl and shell, came together and flew, greater than before. The two in one. One in two. As are our minds.

'Look,' said Kate, 'the world.'

Even so, was it really all over? A dream best forgotten?

'I know, I know,' shouted Kate, jumping up and down in glee, 'we can do it. The t same ship but a NEW NAME!'

' Kate how silly, how could we ever get a name as good as "Pearl of the Seas"'?'

' Well - well, er, Black Pearl?'

'Um,' murmured Chris, creative ever, 'Black, er Black - too short, doesn't really carry you. And a ship has to.'

They fall silent, depressed. Was it really all over?

'I know, I know,' exclaimed Chris suddenly, 'Black inked pearl? Then we could *write* the story of our next adventure. Ink you know... '

'Mm' said Kate a little doubtfully.

'I know,' exclaimed Chris suddenly, 'Black inked pearl'. Then we could *write* the story of our next adventure. Ink you know... '

'Mm,' said Kate a little doubtfully.

'Yes yes, and you'd be the one to do it Kate, you know about black ink writing, all those lines an' all.'

'Um, yes, perhaps. Mmm. And it *will* be a great new adventure won't it Chris. When we're more grown up. Our very own. After all we've proved we really are loyal loving pals, that's why we pulled it off. Hard going some of it, wan it?'

'I'll say.'

'And I tell you what Kate, the next'll be even better, promise.'

'Yes, but not for a few years yet ,' said Kate.

'Actually,' said Chris, ' I think I've grown up a bit! New experiences make you think. Somehow.'

'Not me,' said Kate.

'You're only thirteen of course' (*arrogant, a bit, but only a boy, remember?*).

'But old enough,' said Kate with a cheeky grin.

'I think,' reflected Chris (he'd become almost the many-pondered on his travels), 'we really *were* in heaven you know. Is that possible? That wisdom. And that love. And lions lying down with lambs and everything.'

'Yes, and hell too,' added Kate seriously, ' for me anyway. And learning it was the same thing as well, as just my own fault, and realising it.'

Yes, that was right.

'Do you think we could bring it here too somehow? Heaven I mean,' asked Kate wistfully.

'Well, we could *try*! Our best. And maybe we'll do it. I think the King of Many Names would like that, perhaps he'll help even when he seems so far away. And - and I'll maybe get chosen to take a lead, so I will, however hard that is.'

In his excitement he couldn't help giving Kate a quick hug. After all friendship was another thing the King liked and she really had been a real trusty friend.

'I hope so too,' whispered Kate. 'Do you think we'll get there again. On our next adventure Chris?'

'Yes, and *right* round the world this time. *And* the universe, *all* of it!'

So spoke The Hero. And perhaps he was right.

'Ka-ate. Chris. Teatime ... '

'Help, my mum,' whispered Kate. 'Thank goodness – but is it really the same day?'

'That's what the king said anyway.'

'C'mon darlin's. C'mon then Holly, Ho-ollee.'

A bell was sounding, impatient-like, welcoming-like, across the strand, clear in the misty rain.

Not *that* loud but Holly heard all right. Anything to do with food.

'C'm-o-o-on you two, family tea today, pancakes ready, c'mon before us two eat 'em all up.'

'Better go quick Kate ... tell your mum I'll be ... Oh and - ' Chris's lip trembled before he could stop himself, 'and - and *him*. Is that really right?'

Kate looked at him in surprise.

'Course! They've been friends f'r ever, haven't they, always meant to join up when we got bigger. Easier for cooking an' all.'

'It's all right Kate. I - I think that must have been the surprise the king meant. Best present ever.' He was speaking so quietly that even Holly's sharp ears couldn't catch it.

But Kate heard.

'Love,' said Chris, 'family. The king ... I didn't understand. I thought he'd forgotten about me. Made the queen's present all the better, told myself it was from him too. But now - ,' even more quietly, to himself, 'My dream come true', he whispered.

And Chris couldn't prevent himself giving Kate a quick hug. Holly too.

'You go on Kate. I'll catch you up in a min, mustn't keep them waiting, today of all days. Mm, pancakes, Never had anyone make me those before, bet they're wonderful ... Mustn't get cold.'

And all the bells on earth were ringing.

And all the angels in heaven were singing,

Kate jumped to her feet, looked at Chris and Holly. Hesitated. Big hug for Holly. Then – could she should she? - quick kiss on cheek for Chris, he really was a true friend. Then fled off across the strand.

Chris didn't wipe it off.

'Next time?' he said. Then he ran headlong along the shore after her, the dogs leaping beside him.

' Next time ... '

Well, we shall see …

Ending

Then falter not O book, fulfil your destiny,
You not a reminiscence of the land alone,
You too as a lone bark cleaving the ether, purpos'd I know not
    whither, yet ever full of faith,
Consort to every ship that sails, sail you!
Bear forth to them folded my love, (dear mariners, for you I fold it
    here in every leaf;)
Speed on my book! spread your white sails my little bark athwart the
    imperious waves,
Chant on, sail on, bear o'er the boundless blue from me to every sea,
This song for mariners and all their ships.

Notes

These (optional) notes are not essential for following the story, but can enhance its understanding,

Most of the notes point to the sources that have inspired some of the passages here). Other passages, specially the poems, are from the longer and in some ways more complex novel 'Black Inked Pearl' to which this volume is a kind of prequel (the poems are also published in Kate's separate volume 'Black Ink Poems').

Quotations in double quote marks in the text are from external sources, the rest by the author (Kate).

Chapter 1

'The hero light': Chris must have had an Irish ancestor for it was round the head of the great Celtic warrior Cuchulain that the hero light first shone (you can read more in Lady Gregory's *Cuchulain of Muirthemne : the story of the men of the Red Branch of Ulster*).

.Chapter 2

"How sweet it is ...": Orpheus' song as given in Charles Kingsley, *The Heroes.*

Chapter 3

"Look on this ship ... ": From a poem by the mediaeval Persian poet Rumi.

Chapter 5

Yahwiel is recalling the famous mystical poem by William Blake (1757-1827) 'Auguries of Innocence', the first verse of which runs

To see a World in a grain of sand,
And a Heaven in a wild flower,
Hold Infinity in the palm of your hand,
And Eternity in an hour .

" 'I don't know' is the beginning of wisdom": a celebrated saying by the ancient Greek philosopher Socrates

Chapter 6

"This is oceans poem": from Walt Whitman, *Leaves of Grass.*

Chapter 7

The description of the clashing blue rocks and the ship's passage through is based again on Charles Kingsley's *The Heroes,* a great story book.

The storm descriptions here and elsewhere, so too the account of the Sirens and their song and many echoes throughout, are drawn or adapted from those in Homer's wonderful Greek epic, *The Odyssey* (there are many accessible translations).

Chapter 10

In this chapter the king seems to be recalling, though not quite as we know it (but who can tell which has it right?), the biblical tale of, first, the confusion of the Tower of Babel - the emergence of the many mutually unintelligible languages of earth - then, many centuries later, the reversalat Pentecost (the 'fiftieth day'): all men were still 'speaking in their own tongues' but suddenly, miraculously, understanding each other.

Linguists commonly picture the divisions and development of languages as a kind of tree.

"Dear Lulu ..." : quoted with his blessing from a letter written in April 2011 to 6 yea -old Lulu by Rowan Williams, the 104th Archbishop of Canterbury and Head of the Church of England (accessible on the web).

"As easy might I ... ": from Shakespeare's beautiful sonnet (109) "Oh never say that I was false ... ".

Chapter 11

'Mother's care ca-an reach': 'ca-an' is the evocative Caribbean Creole spelling and pronunciation of 'can't'.

"God be in my head ... ": a much-loved choral blessing dating back to the sixteenth century.

QUESTIONS FOR DISCUSSION

1. What do you think of the style of the book? Does it help or hinder your understanding? How?

2. The same for the illustrations? Why do you think they do or do not help the story along?

3. Which is your favourite picture? Why?

4. Who is the King-of-Many-Names? Have you ever met him, or anyone like him?

5. How does he link up with Yahwiel? Is that important in the story?

6. Was Chris right to be disappointed with the King's farewell present? (would you have been?)

7. Have you or anyone you know ever visited the land of Nowhere-Where (or similar) and if so when? and how?

8. Which character do you like best, and why?

9. Does the book seem to have a kind of 'message'? If so for you personally, or for everyone?

10. What is your favourite fairytale? Does it have anything in common with this one?

11. Is the book too long?

12. Why were all the angels singing?

13. How would you summarise the story to a child a few years younger than you? (let me know if you like, at r.h.finnegan@open.ac.uk)

DEAR READER ...

Thank you for reaching here! I hope that you enjoyed the story.

If you liked it why not look for other of Ruth Finnegan's books on her amazon page or her facebook-author page (www.facebook.com/ruthfinneganauthor/).

Oh and if you wondered what Chris and Kate (and of course Holly) had done earlier a series of children's books (adults might want to sneak a look too) about their adventures are coming soon (a chapter book, and a picture book at least, both with more of Rachel's brilliant pictures – if you'd like to see more of those look at www.rachelbackshall.com).

Oh Kate! A block book

The magic adventure: Kris and Kate build a boat A picture book

Kris and Kate's second magic adventure: the Pearl-Maran A picture story book

The enchanted Pearl-Away A chapter book

The Black Inked Pearl colouring book

As for what they do next, look up the longer novel (all arrived in dreams so must, sort-of, be true) *Black Inked Pearl*, and for another take on this one watch the brilliant 2-minute video about it by Kim of Castelane at https://www.youtube.com/playlist?list=PLPnQyPTu6I0EK0gW61wiEXKjRrLBYLK mL?

Rachel and I would love your thoughts and opinions on *Pearl of the Seas* (send them to me at r.h.finnegan@open.ac.uk) or suggestions for further discussion questions. Or, even better as reaching more people, a review on amazon (maybe because of amazon's silly rules an adult will have to upload), as short as you like – sometimes the briefer the better. See you there!

And why not write your own story, whether about Kate, Holly, Chris or someone else?

Any profits from this book will go to support orphaned children living not in the land of Nowhere-Where but, in full reality in the war-torn uplands of Sierra Leone in West Africa, now thankfully more settled. This is organized though the wonderful charity SOS Children (for further information and updates see http://www.soschildrensvillages.org.uk/

So, in support, do please encourage your friends to buy this and our other books. Please.

Holly sends her thanks too.

Printed in Great Britain
by Amazon

25168136R00066